How to Stop a Train With One Finger

David Henry Wilson was born in London in 1937, and was educated at Dulwich College and Pembroke College, Cambridge. He lectures at the universities of Bristol and Konstanz, West Germany, where he founded the student theatre. He lives in Taunton, Somerset, with his wife and three children. His children's books (including four other books about Jeremy James the irrepressible) have been translated into several languages, and many of his plays have been produced in England and abroad, the best-known being his comedy *Gas and Candles*.

Other books by David Henry Wilson

How to Stop a Train with One Finger

David Henry Wilson

Illustrated by Fred Apps

PIPER BOOKS

First published 1984 by J M Dent & Sons Ltd.
This Piper edition published 1988 by
Pan Books Ltd., Cavaye Place, London SW10 9PG.
9 8 7 6
Text © David Henry Wilson 1984
Illustrations © Fred Apps 1984
ISBN 0 330 28978 0
Phototypeset by Input Typesetting Ltd London
Printed and bound in Great Britain by
Cox & Wyman Ltd, Reading

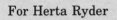

For Herta Ryder

Contents

1 Red between the lines

Jeremy James and Daddy were going on a train journey. It should have been a car journey, but Daddy's car had had one of its coughing and shuddering attacks and was now recovering in the repair shop. Daddy had an appointment in Castlebury, which was fifty miles away, and so while Mummy stayed at home to look after Christopher and Jennifer (she said twin babies weren't much fun on public transport, but Jeremy James thought twin babies weren't much fun anywhere), Daddy and Jeremy James set out to catch the 10.15 train.

By the time Daddy had found his wallet, papers, briefcase and left sock, it was nearly ten o'clock, and Daddy said they would have to run to catch the train. Jeremy James didn't think he could run fast enough to catch any train, but he held on to Daddy's hand, and the two of them

ran-walked and walked-ran all the way to the station.

'Three minutes to go,' said Daddy, puffing like an old steam engine. 'Let's hope the train'll be late.'

They bought the tickets and went panting (Daddy) and scampering (Jeremy James) up a steep slope and on to a long grey platform. This contained a few people and a lot of litter.

'Exactly 10.15!' gasped Daddy. 'Train must be late. Lucky for us.'

At that moment a crackly voice boomed from up in the roof: 'We regret to announce that the 10.15 train to worple, worple, Castlebury, worple, worple and worple is running approximately forty minutes late.'

'Forty minutes!' exclaimed Daddy. 'Ugh, what a service!'

'I thought we *wanted* the train to be late,' said Jeremy James.

'Well yes,' said Daddy, 'but not *too* late!'

Just then there was a distant rattle that grew into a rumble that suddenly became a terrifying roar, and a train hurtled through on the other side of the track. The station and Jeremy James shook like a couple of jellies in a thunderstorm. Then the roar faded to a rumble, a rattle, and finally silence, and the station and Jeremy James stopped shivering.

Jeremy James gazed up the track with a worried expression on his face.

'What's the matter, Jeremy James?' asked Daddy.

'Well,' said Jeremy James, 'if the train's going *that* fast, I don't think I shall be able to get on it.'

Daddy laughed. 'If the train's going,' he said, 'you shouldn't *try* to get on it. You only get on trains that stop.'

At 10.55 the 10.15 train to Castlebury stopped for Daddy and Jeremy James. It came slithering painfully into the station like a giant snake with backache, and Daddy helped Jeremy James up the high steps and into the corridor. They walked along till they found an empty compartment which seemed to be waiting just for them.

'There aren't many people,' said Jeremy James.

'They've probably gone on ahead,' said Daddy. 'On foot.'

Jeremy James sat down by the window, and Daddy sat opposite him. There was a whistle, and the train twitched, jerked, and began to slide gently out of the station.

'We're moving,' said Jeremy James.

'Let us be thankful,' said Daddy, 'for small miracles.'

In the wide frame of the window, houses

and factories and back gardens gave way to fields and trees and rivers. The train diddly-dummed along, and Jeremy James leaned back and looked round the compartment. There was nothing very interesting to see – two pictures of castles, the seat, Daddy, the luggage rack, Daddy's briefcase on the luggage rack. . .and next to Daddy's briefcase a sort of chain.

'Daddy, what's the chain for?' asked Jeremy James.

Daddy followed the direction of Jeremy James's pointing finger.

'Ah, the communication cord,' said Daddy. 'It's so that people can stop the train in an emergency.'

'You mean like wanting to wee?' asked Jeremy James.

That had happened to him once. They'd been driving along the motorway and he'd had an emergency, so Daddy had stopped at the side of the road. Then a police car had come along, and the policeman and Daddy had had a lovely conversation about emergencies.

'No,' said Daddy. 'If it's *that* sort of emergency, there's a lavatory at the end of the corridor.'

A little while later, Daddy himself had *that* sort of emergency, and he went off down the corridor leaving Jeremy James to look out of the window. The train was going quite slowly now, past big gloomy buildings and a lot of railway lines. Perhaps they were coming into a station – one of the worples before Castlebury. Jeremy James hoped Daddy would get back before the train stopped, in case someone wanted to take his seat. But if the worst came to the worst, he could tell them that Daddy was doing an emergency.

It was indeed a station. Jeremy James stood up to get a better view. There were quite a lot of people on the platform, and Jeremy James spotted a crowd of children. The train glided by, and he waved to them. Some of them waved back, and he wished the train would stop just there, but on it went. . .and on. . .and on. And all of a sudden, they were out of the station again! They hadn't stopped at all!

Obviously something had gone wrong. Those people were waiting for the train, but of course they weren't allowed to get on it unless it stopped, and it hadn't stopped. Perhaps the children hadn't been waving to him but to the driver, trying to attract his attention. Perhaps the driver had been looking the wrong way. Or perhaps he was asleep. Or dead. Dead, and slumped over the steering wheel, while the train roared on and on towards disaster and destruction. . .

There was no doubt about it, this was an emergency. Jeremy James leapt on to the seat, clutched the luggage rack with one hand, put one foot on Daddy's arm-rest, heaved himself up, and was just able to reach the communication cord and give it a hearty tug.

Almost at once there was a grinding screech, and it felt as if the train were trying to move backwards while everything inside it tried to move forwards. Jeremy James bounced from arm-rest to seat to floor, and lay there for a moment wondering how much of himself he'd left hanging on the luggage rack. Then he picked himself up, and checked that all of him was still where it was supposed to be. He found that even his nose was still sitting comfortably in the middle of his face, and soon he was pressing it against the window to see if the children and the other passengers were coming.

Wouldn't everybody be pleased! Jeremy James had saved the outside passengers from missing their train, and the inside from disaster. When they found out what had happened, the railway people would probably give him a very big reward.

15

But the children and other passengers didn't come. Daddy came, closely followed by a railway person who had not brought along a big reward. All he brought with him was a peaked cap, a bristly moustache, and a very red face. He didn't seem pleased at all. In fact he was very un-pleased. He said someone had pulled the communication cord, and he wanted to know *who* had pulled the communication cord, and *why* the communication cord had been pulled. Jeremy James explained to him that some people were waiting for this train at the station, and the driver hadn't seen them because he was dead, and so he, Jeremy James, had pulled the communication cord in order to save everybody, and would there be a reward?

The red-faced man's face went redder, and Daddy's face went as red as the red-faced man's had been before it went redder. The people at the station, said the redder-faced man, were not waiting for *this* train, and the driver wasn't dead, and there were two passengers on this train who might end up dead after the driver had heard why his communication cord had been pulled, and there would not be a reward, and grown men should learn to control their children, and there'd already been enough trouble today without. . .

The red-faced man now used a word that Daddy had once used when hammering a nail (his thumbnail) into the wall. Mummy had said that such words were forbidden, but the red-faced man obviously didn't know Mummy had forbidden such words, and after he'd said it twice Daddy went out into the corridor with him, and closed the compartment door.

Jeremy James sat in the corner and looked up at the chain near Daddy's brief-case. It reminded him of when he'd been on a bus with Mummy. Instead of a chain there'd been a bell, and when the conductor wanted the bus to stop or start, he rang the bell. The thought occurred to Jeremy James that maybe if he pulled the chain again, the train might start and the red-faced man would go away.

Jeremy James was just climbing on to Daddy's seat when Daddy came back into the compartment, looking a little sadly at his wallet.

'*Now* what are you up to?' asked Daddy.

Jeremy James explained his idea to Daddy. But Daddy didn't think it was a very good idea.

'Your ideas, Jeremy James,' said Daddy, 'have made a late train later, a red face redder, and poor Daddy a lot poorer. So I

18

think the best idea, Jeremy James, is for you to stop having ideas altogether.'

The train was now moving again, and so Jeremy James sat quietly in the corner and looked out of the window. It wasn't easy to stop having ideas – in fact ideas kept coming to him all the time. He had ideas about ice cream, and chicken, and sweets, and fizzy drinks. He also had an idea about saying he was sorry he'd pulled the communication cord. But he didn't tell Daddy and so Daddy never knew.

2 To be or not to be

Daddy and Jeremy James had lunch in Castlebury. Daddy said he fancied some Chinese food, and Jeremy James said he fancied *any* food, so they went to a Chinese restaurant. Daddy ordered something strange-sounding and strange-looking, and Jeremy James ordered chicken and chips. Chinese chicken and chips looked and tasted just like English chicken and chips, and so did Chinese ice cream and Chinese Coca-Cola.

When lunch was over ('I like Chinese food,' said Jeremy James), they walked through the streets, stopping only to look in a bookshop and nearly to look in a toyshop, until they came to a large building with pillars, posters, photographs, and a crowd of people in the entrance.

Daddy told Jeremy James that this was the theatre, and the people were waiting to see a play. Jeremy James wondered if

they would like to see *him* play, but Daddy didn't think they would. 'Besides,' said Daddy, 'we've got to go and meet a very important man.'

They went past the crowd of people, up a staircase, and into a corridor at the end of which was an open door. Daddy knocked, and poked his head round it.

'Hello, John!' said a cheerful voice from inside.

'Hello, Malcolm,' said Daddy, and he and Jeremy James entered the room. It was a very untidy room with papers, posters, pictures and books everywhere. If Mummy had seen this room, she would have told Malcolm to tidy it immediately.

'This is Jeremy James,' said Daddy. 'Jeremy James, this is Malcolm Crawford who runs the theatre.'

'Hello, Jeremy James,' said Malcolm, who had a sort of upside-down face, with a lot of hair on his chin and none on his head.

'Are you important?' asked Jeremy James.

'Well, I am to me,' said Malcolm. 'Are you important to you?'

'Yes,' said Jeremy James.

'Then we're both important,' said Malcolm. 'Sally!'

22

A fair-haired girl came in from the office next door, and smiled at Jeremy James.

'Now would you two like something to drink?' asked Malcolm.

'No, thanks,' said Daddy. 'We've just had lunch.'

'Yes, please,' said Jeremy James.

It was decided that Jeremy James should go next door with Sally, have his drink, and perhaps do some drawing while Daddy and Malcolm talked about the things they had to talk about. And so off went Jeremy James with Sally, who duly supplied him with his second Coca-Cola, and his first paper and pencil of the day. When Jeremy James had finished eating, drinking, and burping, he sat at a table drawing a train, while Sally sat at her desk and typed letters at ten times the speed of raindrops.

If Sally had continued typing, Jeremy James might well have continued drawing, and the afternoon would have passed quite undramatically. But Sally had to go and see somebody.

'I shan't be long,' she said. 'You'll be all right on your own for a little while, won't you?'

Jeremy James said he would, and he was. For a little while. But the little while grew into a bigger while, and the train was finished, the station was finished, and the red-faced man with a moustache was finished. And drawing was boring anyway. From the office next door he could hear Daddy and Malcolm worpling on, and the thought occurred to him that if people were playing in the theatre, they might let him play with them – at least until Daddy and Malcolm had finished worpling.

Jeremy James opened the door of Sally's office and stepped out into the corridor. It was empty. And so was the staircase, and the next corridor, and the room he peeped into. . .wasn't that a noise from behind the door at the end of the passage? Music, and then voices. Could the people be playing there?

Jeremy James slipped through the door, and found himself in darkness. But there was light further along, and the voices were very clear now – an old man was telling someone to read a book. That didn't sound much fun, but perhaps Jeremy James could persuade them to play something else. Another man was talking now – not quite so old as the first, but not young either. It wasn't going to be easy to play if everyone was old, only whoever was supposed to be reading was sure to be young. Grown-ups are always telling children to read or draw or do something boring.

Jeremy James could see a little more clearly now that his eyes had grown used to the darkness. He was standing behind what looked like walls with gaps between them. The lights and voices were coming from the other side of these walls, and so all he had to do was walk through one of the gaps.

'I hear him coming; let's withdraw, my lord,' said the old man's voice.

That was a surprise. Jeremy James had not realized that anyone knew he was there, but perhaps they were going to play hide-and-seek with him. Quickly he walked through the gap and into the light, hoping to see the old man before he hid. The light was so strong, though, that at first he could see nothing. From beyond the light, which was shining on him from all angles, came a loud murmur, followed by a sort of tittering noise. Then, through a gap in the wall opposite, there came a young man with fair hair, a wispy beard, and the strangest black clothes that Jeremy James had ever seen.

'To be, or not to be,' said the young man. 'That is the question.'

'Hello,' said Jeremy James.

A look of surprise came on to the young

man's face, and there was some loud laughter from beyond the bright lights.

'Get off!' said the young man quietly, without opening his lips.

'Off what?' asked Jeremy James.

'Get off the stage!' hissed the young man.

Jeremy James looked down, but as he didn't seem to be standing on anything in particular, he stayed where he was.

'Why are you wearing those funny clothes?' he asked.

There was now a great roar of laughter from beyond the lights, and Jeremy James screwed up his eyes to try and see who was there. He could just make out some rows

of faces, and they all seemed to be looking in his direction, as if he was a sort of television set.

Jeremy James turned to the young man, who was looking wildly around like someone who's lost a bar of chocolate.

'What are we playing?' asked Jeremy James.

The young man called out: 'Curtain!' which was a game Jeremy James had never heard of, but just at that same moment an old man came in, wearing a long brown robe and a long white beard.

'Ah, 'tis the First Player's son!' said the old man.

'No, I'm not,' said Jeremy James. 'I'm Daddy's son.'

'Come along, my lad,' said the old man, bustling towards Jeremy James. Then to the young man he added: 'My Lord, I'll see that he is safely stowed.'

He put his hand on Jeremy James's arm, and Jeremy James found himself looking up into a face that wasn't a real face at all. It was old, but the lines were not wrinkles – they were drawings in black. And the eyebrows, which had seemed bushy and white from a distance, were not bushy and white in reality – they were fluffed up and painted. And as for the long white beard – Jeremy James had seen a long white beard

27

like that before. It had been at Christmas, and Jeremy James had gone to a party where the Reverend Cole had pretended he was Santa Claus. He'd worn a beard just like this one, and it had fallen off when Jeremy James had shown everyone that this Santa Claus was not the real Santa Claus.

'Are you pretending to be Santa Claus?' Jeremy James asked the old man holding his arm.

The laughter from beyond the lights was now almost as loud as the train that had roared through the station.

'Come along, you little horror!' muttered the old man, and pulled Jeremy James towards a gap in the wall.

Jeremy James didn't like being pulled along by a fake Santa Claus, and somehow, in the struggle the old man got his legs caught in his robe and went tumbling head first down to the ground. This was greeted by a thunderclap of cheering and applause which continued as he clambered to his feet, tucked Jeremy James under one arm, and hurried off through the gap and into the darkness.

Waiting in the darkness were some other shadowy figures that Jeremy James couldn't see properly now that his eyes were used to the bright light.

'Who is he?' whispered one.

'How did he get in?'

'He should be skinned alive!'

'We've got to get rid of him.'

Jeremy James began to find these dark figures and angry mutterings rather frightening, but then he heard a woman's voice that was a little less frightening:

'I'll take him. Give him to me.'

A hand grasped him, and he was led away through the darkness, out of a door, and into a lighted corridor. The lady holding his hand was Sally.

'Oh dear,' said Sally, 'you *are* going to get us into trouble.'

'Why?' asked Jeremy James.

'Because you weren't supposed to go in there,' said Sally. 'And I shouldn't have left you on your own. I'll tell you what. Shall we keep it a secret, just between ourselves?'

'You mean like the price of Mummy's new hat?' asked Jeremy James.

'That's right,' said Sally. 'We'll just pretend you've been in my office all afternoon.'

And so Jeremy James and Sally headed for the office, stopping only to buy a large bar of chocolate at the refreshment counter on the way. Then Sally sat typing, and Jeremy James sat drawing and eating, while Daddy and Malcolm worpled in the office next door.

When Daddy at last poked his head in, Jeremy James had done three drawings and eaten twelve squares of chocolate, and Sally had done twelve letters and eaten three squares of chocolate.

'Time to go, Jeremy James,' said Daddy. 'Sally, how did you manage to keep him so quiet?'

'Oh, I just left him to entertain himself,' said Sally.

Jeremy James said goodbye to Sally, who gave him a kiss, and to Malcolm, who shook his hand, and then he and Daddy went down the staircase and out into the entrance-hall of the theatre. From behind a closed door, Jeremy James could just hear the voice of a woman singing:

'And will he not come again?
And will he not come again?'

'I wonder if she means me,' said Jeremy James.

'And why should she mean you?' asked Daddy.

Jeremy James gave a little smile and took Daddy's hand as they went out of the theatre.

'*That*,' he said, looking back while his legs walked forward, 'is the question.'

3 Eight hairy legs

There was a spider in the bath. Jeremy
James was sitting on the lavatory, and he
just happened to look sideways and downwards, and there was the spider. It wasn't
one of those tiny, tickly ones – he didn't
mind those. No, it was one of those large
leg-spreading ones, black and hairy and
shuddery – the sort that make your back-
bone run up and down your body.

It's not easy to think about other things
when there's a black spider sprawling less
than three feet away from your bare legs.
At any moment it could come scrabbling
up the bath and on to your foot, legs,
tummy. . . ugh! Besides, where there's one
spider there could be other spiders, and
there's just no telling where they might
crawl to. Jeremy James immediately felt
a goose-pimply tingle at the back of his
neck, and slapped it hard to make sure the
goose-pimple didn't creep down on to his

back. Then the thought occurred to him
that if a spider got into the bath, another
spider might get into the lavatory, and
then just think where that could creep to!
He leapt off the seat and looked into the
pan. Nothing.

He looked down into the bath again, just
in time to see the spider take a quick
scuttly step towards the plughole. Then it
stopped still again, legs slightly bent, as if
tensed to do a mighty leap. If it leapt out
of the bath, Jeremy James decided he
would leap out of the bathroom. But what
should he do if it stayed in the bath?

Jeremy James remembered a spider that had once been hanging on his bedroom wall. He had known then that he'd never be able to sleep while it was there, and so he'd taken his bedroom slipper and given the spider a whack. But the result had been a horrible mess. Half the spider had been squelched into the wall, and the other half had been squelched into the slipper, and Mummy had had to come and wipe all the bits and pieces away with a wet cloth. Even then, Jeremy James hadn't slept very well, because he kept imagining spider-legs running all over him.

On another occasion he'd called for Daddy, and Daddy had arrived with a large sheet of newspaper.

'Let's have a look then,' Daddy had said, and with the newspaper spread wide he had advanced on the spider and had suddenly jammed the paper against the wall and at great speed screwed it up into a big ball.

'He won't trouble you any more,' Daddy had said. 'He's either dead or studying the sports news.'

But Jeremy James had seen something Daddy had not seen, and he asked Daddy to unscrew the paper again. And when Daddy unscrewed the paper, he found to his surprise that there was nothing there except the sports news. Then they had spent half an hour trying in vain to attract a spider that clearly wasn't interested in sport. That had been another sleepless night.

Well, at least this was morning, and the spider was in the bathroom, not the bedroom. But the problem was the same – how do you get rid of a spider without making it into a mess or a magic vanishing act?

The spider twitched and twiddled itself one step nearer the plughole. Jeremy James had an idea. Another few steps and it would be near enough for him to turn the tap on and swoosh it away down the hole. No mess at all. In fact, as clean an end as you could wish for.

'Move!' said Jeremy James. 'Go on! Shoo! Quick march!'

The spider did not even slow-march. Jeremy James stood and looked at the spider, and the spider stood and looked at Jeremy James. This was not going to be easy. Jeremy James needed a weapon, and his eye fell on the bathbrush. A scratch with those bristles should make even the toughest spider jump. It might even take the brush for a monster with a moustache and die of fright.

Jeremy James ran the bathbrush along

the bottom of the bath, until the bristles were almost touching what might be the spider's eighth little toenail. The spider remained very still. Jeremy James moved the brush again so that it just touched the tip of the spidery toe. The spider twitched. Probably thought it had an itch. Jeremy James pushed the brush firmly against the spider's leg. With a scurry and a flurry the spider raced forward, while Jeremy James leapt back and dropped the brush in the bath with a clatter.

Now his heart was jumping like a grasshopper with hiccups. This was turning out to be a dangerous battle. In the past he'd killed snakes and crocodiles and maneating tigers in the bath, but none of them had given him half as much trouble as this spider. There it lurked, hairy legs spread wide apart, waiting to pounce and cover him with shivers. Two inches away from the plughole.

Gradually Jeremy James's heart sat down again in his chest. If he could just push the spider with the brush and then whoosh it with the tap, he could send it sailing down the Seven Seas. On the other hand, it might grab hold of the brush and come racing over the bristles, handle, hand, arm. . .

Heroes don't think about might-be's.

Jeremy James leaned over the bath, picked up the brush, and with eyes swivelling like tennis-watchers he reached for the tap nearest the spider.

Swoosh and sweep! Down came the water and the brush, and as the spider struggled to swim up the bath, so Jeremy James pushed it down again. But the flow of water kept bringing the spider back up the bath again. Jeremy James turned the tap off, and the water sucked the spider back towards the hole.

'Down you go!' said Jeremy James.

And with eight despairing waves and a loud gurgle, the spider disappeared from view.

Bathbrush in hand, Jeremy James stood triumphant.

'Jeremy James!' came Mummy's voice from the landing. 'Haven't you finished in there?'

'I've just been killing a spider,' said Jeremy James.

'Well hurry up. I'm waiting to bath the twins!' called Mummy.

'It was a huge spider!' said Jeremy James. 'And it nearly killed *me*!'

But Mummy didn't seem interested. Perhaps she might have been more interested if the spider *had* killed Jeremy James. Then she might have wished she'd thought more about spiders and less about baths and twins.

Jeremy James sat down on the lavatory again, legs dangling and lips pouting. What was the use of being a hero if nobody was interested? He glanced sadly down at the scene of his heroism – and his glance got stuck into a long and disbelieving stare: there, on the edge of the plughole, looking a little damp and dazed and drippy, was the ghost of the drowned spider.

Jeremy James leapt off the lavatory as if it had been a pin-cushion. 'Mummy!' he cried.

'What is it?' asked Mummy from one of the bedrooms.

'There's a spider in the bath!' cried Jeremy James.

'I thought you'd killed it,' said Mummy, now on the landing.

Jeremy James unlocked the bathroom door, and Mummy came in.

'Ugh!' she said. 'What a monster!'

'I did kill it,' said Jeremy James, 'but it must have unkilled itself.'

'Well, this is what we do with spiders,' said Mummy. On the bathroom shelf, next to the toothbrush stand, was the mouthwash glass, which Mummy picked up in her right hand. With her left, she tore off a sheet of toilet paper. 'Now watch carefully,' she said.

Then she bent over the bath, and put the glass upside down round the spider. She slid the sheet of paper under the glass and under the spider, turned the glass the right way up, and plop! There was the spider sitting at the bottom of the glass.

'He doesn't look quite so big now, does he?' said Mummy, holding the glass so that Jeremy James could see.

In fact the spider seemed quite small and silly, sitting there looking out at Jeremy James looking in.

'What shall we do with him?' asked Mummy.

'Can we throw him out of the window?' suggested Jeremy James.

'Good idea,' said Mummy.

She opened the window, leaned out, and with a flick of her wrist sent the spider diving down to the lawn below. Then she showed Jeremy James the empty glass, which she washed out and replaced on the bathroom shelf.

'And now,' said Mummy, 'perhaps you'll do what you're supposed to be doing.'

Mummy left the bathroom, and Jeremy James perched on the lavatory again. It was amazing how simple things were when

Mummy did them. He looked all round the bathroom, hoping to see another spider so that he could do the trick with the glass and paper. But there wasn't a spider to be seen.

There was just one thing about Mummy's trick that slightly worried Jeremy James. It was nothing very important, but when a little later he cleaned his teeth, he rinsed his mouth with water straight from the tap. He didn't really need a glass for that anyway.

4 Campers

Mummy was changing Christopher's nappy when the front doorbell rang.

'Jeremy James, would you please see who it is!' called Mummy from upstairs, and Jeremy James stood on tip-toe to open the front door. Standing on the step were Mrs Smyth-Fortescue from next door, and her son Timothy, who was a year older than Jeremy James and knew all about everything.

'Hello, Jeremy,' said Mrs Smyth-Fortescue, who never called him Jeremy *James*. 'Is your mummy in?'

'Yes, Mrs Smyth-Forciture,' said Jeremy James, who never said Smyth-*Fortescue*, 'but Christopher's just done a pong.'

'Ah, she's changing him, is she?' asked Mrs Smyth-Fortescue.

'No,' said Jeremy James, 'I think she's going to keep him.'

Mummy came down the stairs. 'Hello,

Mrs Smyth-Fortescue,' she said. 'Won't you come in?'

'No, we can't stop,' said Mrs Smyth-Fortescue. 'We just popped round to see if Jeremy would like to spend the night in Timothy's new tent. We bought it yesterday – frightfully expensive, but his old one was falling to bits, and he did so want this new one. It's the best on the market.'

'I'm sure he'd like to,' said Mummy.

'Jeremy's such good company for Timothy,' said Mrs Smyth-Fortescue. 'And they get on so nicely together.'

Timothy looked at Jeremy James and held his nose, and Jeremy James poked out his tongue at Timothy.

'Would you like that, Jeremy James?' asked Mummy.

'Ugh. . .hmmph. . .well. . .' said Jeremy James.

'Timothy doesn't want to sleep there on his own,' said Mrs Smyth-Fortescue, 'and I'm. . .well, ha ha. . .a little past such things, you know. My husband would keep Timothy company, but he's away on business. In America this time. Such a bore.'

'You'd love to sleep in Timothy's tent, wouldn't you, Jeremy James?' asked Mummy.

'Hmmph. . .well. . .ugh. . .' said Jeremy James.

'Oh good, I'm so glad,' said Mrs Smyth-Fortescue. 'Then that's settled. The tent's already up in the back garden, and I'll cook them a lovely barbecue supper. Do you like sausages, Jeremy?'

'Well, yes,' said Jeremy James.

'And baked beans and chips?'

Jeremy James did like baked beans and chips, and he liked sausages, and he liked the idea of sleeping in a tent. It was just a pity that Timothy would have to be there as well.

'Good,' said Mrs Smyth-Fortescue. 'We'll see you later, Jeremy.'

'Yes, Mrs Smyth-Torcyfue,' said Jeremy James.

'Big pong,' said Timothy.

'And so are you,' said Jeremy James.

The new tent was a beauty. It was high enough for the boys to stand in, and apart from the two airbeds, one on either side of the central pole, there was even room for a little table and two little chairs. And here they sat as Mrs Smyth-Fortescue served them with sausages, baked beans and chips, Coca-Cola and ice cream. She

43

left them gobbling like a couple of starved turkeys, and for minutes on end there was no sound but contented munching, slurping and burping.

When eventually they had finished, Jeremy James put his dessert plate on his dinner plate, and his glass on his dessert plate, and sat back feeling rather pleased with life.

'You've never been camping before!' said Timothy.

Jeremy James felt slightly less pleased with life. 'Hmmph!' he said.

'Real campers don't put their dishes like that,' said Timothy. 'Anybody who knows anything about camping knows you don't put dishes like that!'

'Well, how do you put dishes, then?' asked Jeremy James.

'You leave them – like this,' said Timothy, indicating his own dishes spread out over the table.

'My mummy says you should put your dishes like this!' said Jeremy James, indicating his neat little pile.

'Then your mummy doesn't know anything about camping either,' said Timothy.

Just then Mrs Smyth-Fortescue arrived to collect the dirty dishes. 'Oh, what a good boy, Jeremy,' she said. 'Piling up your dishes so nicely.'

'My mother's never been camping either,' said Timothy, when Mrs Smyth-Fortescue had gone. 'It's only men who know about camping.'

'You're not a man,' said Jeremy James.

'I will be soon,' said Timothy. 'Much sooner than you.'

'Well if you're such a man,' said Jeremy James, 'why were you scared to sleep in the tent on your own?'

'Scared?' said Timothy. 'SCARED??? Me??? I'll show you who's scared!'

Whereupon he hurled himself at Jeremy James, and as he was much bigger and heavier, it was not long before he was sitting on Jeremy James's chest, with his knees pinning Jeremy James's arms to the ground.

'Now who's scared?' asked Timothy, scowling down.

'Just because you're bigger than me,' said Jeremy James, 'it doesn't prove you're not. . .ouch!'

Timothy had leaned forward, squashing Jeremy James's head with his chest.

'Having a nice game, dears?' came the voice of Mrs Smyth-Fortescue. 'You'd better go to the bathroom now, before it gets really dark. Timothy, get off Jeremy.'

'Can't,' said Timothy.

'Come along, Jeremy,' said Mrs Smyth-Fortescue. 'Let Timothy get off now.'

Eventually Mrs Smyth-Fortescue made Jeremy James let go of Timothy's knees with his arms, and release Timothy's bottom from his chest, and the two boys went to the house to wash their hands and faces, and clean their teeth. But Timothy didn't wash and didn't clean his teeth, because he said campers never did.

By the time they were tucked up in bed, the night was as black as Timothy's knees. Mrs Smyth-Fortescue had left them a torch which Timothy said only he should have,

because he was the one that knew about camping. He shone it a few times in Jeremy James's eyes, but then he began to shine it round the tent, and the beam came to rest on the door-flap. 'Do you think a lion could get through the door?' he asked.

'I expect so,' said Jeremy James. 'Your mother got in, didn't she?'

'My mother's not a lion,' said Timothy.

'She's the same size as a lion,' said Jeremy James. 'But a bit fatter.'

There was a moment's silence. The torch continued to shine on the flap.

'A ghost could get in, too,' said Timothy.

'Ghosts can get in anywhere,' said Jeremy James. 'Ghosts can even get in to your bedroom. And so can spiders.'

'Ugh!' said Timothy.

There was a noise outside the tent – a padding noise.

'What's that?' came Timothy's terrified whisper.

'I don't know,' whispered Jeremy James. 'Put the light out, so it won't know we're here!'

Timothy switched off the torch. There was more padding, then a snuffle-whiffle-snort, then silence. Then more silence.

'Has it gone?' whispered Timothy.

'Don't know,' whispered Jeremy James.

More silence. No more padding. No more snuffles. WHOO WHOO!

'W... w... wa... what's that?' Timothy's voice came out in a hoarse wobble.

'That's an owl,' said Jeremy James. 'No need to be scared of an owl!'

WHOO WHOO! WHOO WHOO!

'S...sou...sounds like a g...gug ...ghost to me,' said Timothy.

'Ghosts say BOO, not WHOO,' said Jeremy James.

'S...s...some gug...gug...ghosts s... say WHOO!' said Timothy.

But boo-saying and whoo-saying ghosts didn't really matter any more to Jeremy James. The weight of the sausages, beans and chips had begun to shift from his tummy to his eyes, and when his eyes closed, his ears closed, too. Only his imagination stayed awake, supplying him with dreams of Mrs Smyth-Fortescue roaring on all fours, and of himself being pinned to the ground by a string of sausages.

When Jeremy James woke up the next morning, he was surrounded by a glow of orange and green, which he soon realized was the sun shining into the tent and on to the grass. The other thing he soon realized was that Timothy's bed and sleeping bag were still there, and Timothy's clothes were still there, but Timothy himself was most definitely not there.

Perhaps, thought Jeremy James with a little smile, a lion had gobbled Timothy up in the night. Or a ghost might have taken him off to the Land of Shivers. Anyway, he had better tell Mrs Smyth-Fortescue. He wasn't sure whether Mrs Smyth-Fortescue would be glad or sorry that Timothy had disappeared, but she would certainly want to know.

Jeremy James stepped out of the tent and on to the lawn.

'Hello, Jeremy!' called Mrs Smyth-Fortescue through the open kitchen window. 'Did you sleep well?'

'Yes, thank you, Mrs Smyth-Forkystew,' said Jeremy James.

'I suppose Timothy's still asleep,' she said.

'I don't know,' said Jeremy James.

'You don't know?' said Mrs Smyth-Fortescue.

'Well, he's not there,' said Jeremy James.

'Not there?' echoed Mrs Smyth-Fortescue. 'Then where is he?'

'Well, we did hear a lion in the night,' said Jeremy James, 'so with a bit of luck. . .'

'Let's see if he's in his bedroom,' said Mrs Smyth-Fortescue.

So Jeremy James entered the house, and he and Mrs Smyth-Fortescue went upstairs to Timothy's bedroom. And there on the bed, totally uneaten and very asleep, lay Timothy.

'Wake up, dear!' said Mrs Smyth-Fortescue. 'Timothy, wake up!'

Timothy woke up. His eyes woke up first, and then his brain woke up second, and he sat up in surprise at the sight of his mother and Jeremy James.

'What are you doing here, dear?' asked Mrs Smyth-Fortescue. 'You were supposed to be in the tent with Jeremy.'

'Oh. . .ugh. . .um. . .er. . .' said Timothy.

'What was that, dear?' said Mrs Smyth-Fortescue.

'Um. . .ugh. . .' said Timothy.

'Why aren't you in the tent, dear?' asked Mrs Smyth-Fortescue.

Timothy looked hard at the wall. Then he looked at the floor. And then at the bed.

'Um. . .I had a tummy ache. That's it, I had a tummy ache in the night. I had a tummy ache, so I had to come in.'

'Oh, what a shame,' said Mrs Smyth-Fortescue. 'It must have been all those sausages and beans. What a pity! And you were so looking forward to sleeping in the tent, weren't you, darling?'

'Yes, I was,' said Timothy. 'Only I had a tummy ache.'

'Well, it was very brave and sensible of you to come back here, then, dear,' said Mrs Smyth-Fortescue.

'Yes, I know,' said Timothy. 'I came back because I had a tummy ache.'

Timothy's tummy ache didn't stop him from eating a large breakfast of cornflakes, egg and bacon, and toast and marmalade. Jeremy James (who also had a large breakfast) did suggest to Timothy that perhaps people with tummy aches shouldn't be able to eat such large breakfasts, but Timothy said all campers had large breakfasts, and if Jeremy James had been a *real* camper, he'd have known that.

'A real camper,' said Jeremy James, with his mouth full of toast and marmalade, 'would know an owl isn't a ghost, and a real camper wouldn't get tummy ache in the night, and a real camper. . . a *real* camper. . .' continued Jeremy James, looking straight at Timothy, 'a *really* real camper wouldn't go to bed in his bedroom.'

Timothy munched his toast and marmalade, and for once he didn't say a word.

5 Small talk

There was a new arrival at the house. Jeremy James thought it was a marvellous new toy, Mummy thought it was very useful, and Daddy thought it was a worple worple nuisance. It was called a telephone.

One of the first calls was for Daddy, who was in the bath at the time. With the bath towel draped round his dripping body, he came paddling downstairs, arriving just as Mummy put the phone down.

'He'll ring back in half an hour,' said Mummy.

In fact he rang back in a quarter of an hour, which brought Daddy paddle-dripping down again. That was the first time Daddy called the phone a worple worple nuisance.

Jeremy James listened while Mummy rang a shop, but nothing special happened. She asked when they were open, was told

the answer and rang off. But Daddy's tele-
phoning was rather different.

'I'll save myself a trip into town,' said
Daddy. 'I'll ring the Post Office and find out
the cost of an airmail letter to America.'

'Can I dial the number, please, Daddy?'
asked Jeremy James.

'Why not?' said Daddy. 'Put your finger
here. Now, dial 7—4—4—3—1.'

With the receiver at his ear, Jeremy
James listened to the whirring of the
numbers, and when he had finished he
could hear a brrr brrr sound at the other
end.

'I'd better take it now,' said Daddy.

Jeremy James heard someone say,
'Hello', and then Daddy said: 'Good
morning. Could you please tell me the cost
of an airmail letter to America?'

The voice at the other end said something indistinct, and then Daddy said:
'Sorry, I must have got a wrong number,'
and put the phone down. 'You must have
dialled wrong,' Daddy said to Jeremy
James, and so Daddy dialled the number
himself, got the same person again, and
this time said he was extremely sorry.
Then he looked in the phone book and
found he'd chosen the number above the
one he ought to have chosen. With the new
number he got through to the Post Office,

and was told he needed 'Enquiries'. 'Ah,' said Daddy, 'now we're getting somewhere!'

But 'Enquiries' said he needed 'Counter Services', and from 'Counter Services' there was nothing but brrr brrr.

'Probably gone for coffee,' said Daddy, putting the phone down with a bang and a tinkle.

'Or having a bath,' said Mummy.

That was the second time Daddy called the phone a worple worple nuisance.

Jeremy James wondered how people could make themselves small enough to get inside the phone, but Daddy explained that they didn't. They just sent their voices down the wire. Jeremy James pointed out that voices didn't have legs, and Daddy explained that they didn't need legs, because it was just a matter of soundwaves being what's-a-named into thingamies. Jeremy James didn't understand the what's-a-names or the thingamies, and so Daddy said: 'Well, that's how it is,' and so that was how it was.

What Jeremy James really wanted, far more than explanations of what's-a-names and thingamies, was the chance to make a phone call of his own. His chance came that same afternoon, when Daddy had gone to the Post Office to find out the cost of an airmail letter to America. Mummy and the twins were having a nap, and Jeremy James was supposed to be playing with his trains or his space machine or his farmyard. Of course, Mummy and Daddy had said he shouldn't touch the telephone, but what harm could come if he was careful not to drop it? And he would be *very* careful. He would hold the telephone as carefully as he would hold Christopher or Jennifer or a piece of chocolate.

Jeremy James picked up the telephone, which purred like a pussy-cat. He dialled a number. There was the same whirring sound as before. He dialled another number – and another, and another, and another, until...brrr brrr, brrr brrr. Jeremy James smiled with pleasure and excitement. Would it be Mummy's shop, or the Post Office, or...

'Hello,' said an elderly lady's voice at the other end.

'Hello,' said Jeremy James.

'Who is it?' asked the lady.

'It's me,' said Jeremy James.

'Who's me?' asked the lady.

'Jeremy James,' said Jeremy James.

'Who do you want to speak to, Jeremy James?' asked the lady.

'Well, you, if you don't mind,' said Jeremy James.

'Me?' said the lady. 'No, I don't mind – if you're sure it's me you want to speak to.'

'Quite sure,' said Jeremy James. 'I've just dialled your number.'

'Ah,' said the lady, 'that must be why my telephone rang.'

'It's lucky you answered it,' said Jeremy James.

'Why's that?' asked the lady.

'Because if you hadn't,' said Jeremy James, 'I wouldn't have been able to speak to you.'

'That's true,' said the lady. 'Now tell me, Jeremy James, what have you been doing with yourself?'

'Well, Daddy's out and Mummy and the twins are asleep, so I'm all on my own with boring trains and things,' said Jeremy James. 'What have *you* been doing?'

'I'm all on my own, too,' said the lady. 'So I was knitting some clothes for my grandchildren.'

'Knitting!' cried Jeremy James. 'That's even more boring than trains!'

'There's not much else for me to do,' said the lady.

'No, there's not much else for me to do either,' said Jeremy James. 'Are your grandchildren asleep, too?'

'Oh no, they don't live here,' said the lady. 'I live alone.'

'Haven't you got a husband?' asked Jeremy James.

There was a little stretch of silence at the other end of the wire, and then the lady told Jeremy James that her husband had died six months ago. Her voice seemed suddenly to have a sort of knot tied in it. Jeremy James said he was sorry her husband had died, because that meant her husband wouldn't come back, would he?

'No, he won't come back,' said the lady sadly. 'And that's why I have to live alone.'

'Can I come and visit you one day?' asked Jeremy James.

'That would be lovely,' said the lady, 'but you don't know where I live, do you?'

'I could walk along the telephone wire,' said Jeremy James.

'I think it might be easier if I told you my name and address,' said the lady. 'Then perhaps your Mummy and Daddy could bring you for tea one day.'

Then she told Jeremy James her name which was Mrs Small, and her address, which was 4 Silver Street, Netherton, Carlisle. Jeremy James repeated it several times so that he wouldn't forget it.

'Now, can you tell me your address?' asked the lady, and when Jeremy James told her, she let out a loud gasp. 'You're right down in the south!' she said. 'And I'm right up in the north! Oh dear, this call is going to cost you a lot of money!'

'No, it doesn't cost anything,' said Jeremy James. 'I just picked the phone up and dialled.'

'I'm afraid it's your Daddy who'll have to pay,' said the lady, 'and he won't be very pleased. We'd better ring off, Jeremy James – but thank you for a really lovely chat.'

They said goodbye to each other, then there was a click and the pussy-cat noise, which meant they couldn't talk any more.

Two days later, the front-doorbell rang, and standing on the step was the postman with a big brown parcel for Jeremy James.

Mummy brought the parcel into the living-room, and helped Jeremy James untie the string. Inside the brown paper was a box, and inside the box was. . .

'It's a walkie-talkie!' said Jeremy James.

'So it is!' said Mummy. 'Now who could have sent you that? Ah, there's a card.'

Jeremy James opened the card, and Mummy read it out to him:

*'I hope that you'll be pleased to get
This little walkie-talkie set.
Perhaps when to your friends you call,
You'll sometimes think of Mrs Small.'*

'Who's Mrs Small?' asked Mummy.

'She's the lady I spoke to on the telephone,' said Jeremy James.

'When was that?' asked Mummy.

'When you and the twins were asleep,' said Jeremy James.

'Oh, it was a wrong number, was it?' said Mummy. 'Good heavens, look at the address! Carlisle! That's a long way to dial a wrong number. How did show know your name and address, then, Jeremy James?'

'I told her,' said Jeremy James. 'We had a little chat.'

'Ah well,' said Mummy. 'I'm glad *we* shan't have to pay for your little chat!'

'Hmmph,' said Jeremy James, and buried his nose in the parcel.

6   The gerbil

Richard was one of Jeremy James's best friends. He was a fat boy with a round red face, a round red mother, a tall thin father, and a short thin grandmother. They all lived across the road, down the end of the street, and round the corner at No 24. Sometimes Richard came to play with Jeremy James, and sometimes Jeremy James went to play with Richard. On this particular day it was Jeremy James who went to Richard.

'Come and see what I've got!' said Richard, his apple cheeks shining with pleasure.

Up to his room they went, and there on a table next to the wardrobe was a large white cage. Inside the cage, digging its way through a pile of sawdust and shredded paper was. . .

'It's a mouse!' said Jeremy James.

'No it's not,' said Richard. 'It's a gerbil.'

'A whattle?'

'A gerbil!' said Richard. 'It's just like a mouse, only different. Isn't it great!'

'Yes,' said Jeremy James. 'I wish I had one. What's it called?'

'Jerry,' said Richard. 'Or if it's a girl, Jenny.'

'My sister's Jenny,' said Jeremy James, 'only I'd sooner have a gerbil.'

'Would you like to hold it?' asked Richard.

'Oh!' said Jeremy James. 'Could I?'

'Yes,' said Richard. 'It's lovely to hold.'

Richard undid the hook on the door and reached into the cage.

'Come on, Jerry,' he said. 'This way.'

And when he turned towards Jeremy James, there was the gerbil cupped in the palm of his right hand, while his left hand gently stroked the little brown head.

'Now hold him firmly,' said Richard, 'but not too tight or you'll squash him.'

'All right,' said Jeremy James.

He held out his hand, and gave a little squeak of excitement as Richard gently lowered the gerbil on to his palm. It was the tingliest feeling. The little furry body nestled in his fingers, and he could feel its tiny movements as it breathed and tried to wriggle. Jeremy James found himself going goose-pimply all over.

'Nice, isn't it?' said Richard.

'Yes,' said Jeremy James. 'I wish *I* had a gerbil.'

'Richard!' It was the voice of Richard's mother from downstairs. 'Gran wants you!'

'She would!' said Richard. 'She always wants me to do things when I'm doing other things. Hold Jerry; I'll be back in a minute.'

He clumped downstairs, and soon clumped upstairs again with the news that Gran wanted him to go to the library.

'Will you come with me?' he asked.

'All right,' said Jeremy James. 'Can I bring Jerry?'

'So long as you hold him tight,' said Richard. 'But not too tight.'

Off they went, with Richard holding a bag full of books, and Jeremy James holding a hand full of gerbil. When they reached the library, Richard handed the books to a lady at the counter, and then gave her a list of the new books Gran wanted. The librarian smiled at the two boys, and went to fetch the new books.

'I don't know why Gran wants all these books,' said Richard. 'She never reads them, 'cos she's always alseep. The only time she isn't asleep is when she's making me do things for her.'

'We've got a lot of books at home,' said Jeremy James. 'I think Mummy uses them to trap dust.'

As he spoke, Jeremy James's mind wandered to the books in the living-room, and so it forgot to send certain important messages to his fingers. The fingers loosened their grip on the gerbil inside them, and wriggle, squeeze, plop, scurry – away it scampered across the library floor.

'Oh dear!' said Jeremy James.

'What's the matter?' asked Richard.

'There goes Jerry!' said Jeremy James.

With mouths gaping like cage doors, the boys watched the gerbil disappear into the reading-room.

'We'd better go and get him,' said Richard, 'before someone treads on him.'

They headed towards the reading-room, but before they had even reached the door, there was a terrified scream from within.

'Aaaaaaargh! It's a mouse!'

Then there came a chorus of screams, chairs went flying, one woman clambered on to a table, another ran howling out of the room, and an elderly man with a pointed moustache started waving his walking stick in the air and shouting: 'Where is it? Where's the brute?'

By the time Richard and Jeremy James had timidly crept through the doorway, two more women had climbed on to the tables, and a third sat rigidly in her chair, crying: 'Save me! Save me!' Of Jerry there was no sign, which was a good thing because the owner of the moustache and stick was prowling round the room shouting: 'Where's the beast? I'll soon kill it!'

'Please don't kill him!' cried Richard. 'He's my pet gerbil!'

But nobody heard him above the screams of the women and the war cries of the moustache.

Jeremy James got down on his hands and knees. 'Jerry!' he cried. 'Come on, boy! Come on, Jerry! Or Jenny!'

Suddenly he saw a flash of brown in one

corner as the gerbil disappeared behind a bookcase. At that moment the moustache was in the opposite corner, shouting: 'Come on out, you coward!'

'What's going on in here?' came a stern voice from the doorway. Jeremy James peeped out from under a table, and saw a man with a red face and bristles. 'What's all the fuss?' he was asking.

'Damned mouse on the rampage,' said the moustache.

'Save me! Save me!' cried the rigid woman.

'Help! Mouse! Help! Aaaaargh!' cried the other women.

'It's not a mouse,' said Richard, still standing by the door, 'it's my pet gerbil.' And he began to cry.

'I know where he is,' said Jeremy James from under his table. 'I'm sure I can get him out.'

The chief librarian looked redly and bristly down at Jeremy James. 'Get him out, then,' he ordered, 'and be quick about it.'

Jeremy James crawled swiftly across the room, like a cat in short trousers, and pressed himself up against the wall at the end of the bookcase. With one eye he could just see along the gap at the back, and nestling there in the shadow was the unmistakable shape of a tiny trembling gerbil.

By now the moustache had stopped waving the stick, the rigid woman had stopped asking to be saved, and the women on the tables had stopped screaming. As Jeremy James lay on the floor and squeezed his arm round behind the book-case, the only sound to be heard was the quiet sniffle-snuffle of Richard.

'Got him!' said Jeremy James.

A sigh went round the reading-room.

Jeremy James stood up, firmly holding the gerbil in one hand and stroking it with the other.

'Well done, lad,' said the moustache. 'Damned fine show!'

'Has it gone? Has it gone?' asked the rigid woman.

'It's only a little gerbil,' said Jeremy James, and just to show her how little it was, he stood beside her and took his stroking hand off Jerry's head.

The rigid woman took one look, gasped like a punctured tyre, slumped white-faced back in her chair, and fell fast asleep.

'Get out of here!' growled the bristly man, 'and don't you ever bring that animal in here again!'

Richard and Jeremy James left the

reading-room almost as fast as Jerry had entered it.

'Here are your books,' said the lady at the counter.

'Thank you,' said Richard, as he stuffed the books into his bag, and wobble-rushed out of the library as fast as his jellied legs could carry him. Jeremy James and the gerbil were right behind him.

A little old lady who was returning her books at the counter watched them go. 'How nice,' she said, 'to see children so eager to read.'

7 The mess

'Just look at this mess!' said Mummy.

Jeremy James looked at the mess.

'Have you ever seen anything like it?' asked Mummy.

Jeremy James had often seen something like it. He saw something like it every day. The only time his room wasn't like it was when Mummy came in and made him un-mess it.

'I've lost count,' said Mummy, 'of the number of times I've tidied your room — and as fast as I tidy it, you untidy it. Look at your bed.'

Jeremy James looked at his bed.

'I don't mind the teddy,' said Mummy, 'but a racing car, a lorry, a gun, a book . . . and what's this sweet wrapper doing here?'

'Well, it's. . .sort of. . .lying there. . .' said Jeremy James.

'I don't know how you can sleep in the middle of all this,' said Mummy. 'Anyway,

I want it all tidy. I've brought you a nice big box to put your toys in, and you can put the rubbish in this bin. Right?'

'Yes, Mummy,' said Jeremy James.

'And don't forget to do under the bed!'

'No, Mummy.'

Out went Mummy, and down sat Jeremy James. Tidy, tidy, tidy. What was the point in putting toys away? Toys were for playing with, not for putting away. It was only because grown-ups didn't play with toys that they wanted toys to be put away. Anyone who did play with toys knew that you couldn't play with toys that were stuck in boxes.

From downstairs came the faint sound of Mummy's voice: 'John, I do wish you'd keep your study tidier. I've never seen such a mess. . .'

Then a door shut, and Jeremy James couldn't hear any more.

Jeremy James looked at the box Mummy had brought. It was a big cardboard box with a picture of bananas on the side. You could sit in a box like that. You could make it into a boat, or tank, or plane. You could put sweets in it. Or even bananas. What a waste to put toys in a box like that!

Tidy, tidy, tidy. The bin was just a plain old tin bin. You could put it over your head, or bang it like a drum. Or put rubbish in it. What rubbish? The sweet wrapper perhaps – he wouldn't need that any more. It had once been a toffee – the best sort of toffee, hard and chewy and tooth-sticky. Now just a sweet memory.

Jeremy James carried the wrapper across to the bin, took careful aim, and let it fall. It floated sadly down, on to the carpet.

'Missed!' said Jeremy James.

He left it there. If it didn't want to go in, it didn't want to go in.

Jeremy James wandered across the room and looked out of the window. Perhaps there would be a message in the sky: Thou shalt not tidy or throw things away. But instead he saw the postman padding up the path. Could that mean another parcel from Mrs Small?

Jeremy James raced downstairs in time to see a letter squeeze through the flap and flop down into the hall. He picked it up. One flat letter. Too flat even to contain a stick of chewing gum.

Mummy emerged from the kitchen.

'There's a letter, Mummy,' said Jeremy James, holding it up and hoping Mummy would say: 'There's a good boy. Now you needn't bother with the tidying.'

'Thank you,' said Mummy, drying her hands on her apron. 'And how's the tidying going?'

'Well. . .hmmph. . .' said Jeremy James.

Mummy looked at the letter. 'Bill,' she said.

'Who's Bill?' asked Jeremy James.

'Electricity bill,' said Mummy.

And then there was a bang and a crash and a rude word from Daddy's study.

'What's Daddy doing?' asked Jeremy James.

'Tidying,' said Mummy. 'Off you go.'

Jeremy James dragged himself towards the stairs.

'Mummy,' he said, 'can I just have a little drink?'

'When you've put all your things away,' said Mummy, and went back into the kitchen.

Jeremy James was suddenly dying of thirst. Step by painful step he heaved himself up the stairs, like a cowboy heaving himself across the desert. Mummy would probably tell the cowboy: 'You can have your drink when you've put all the sand away.' Mummy was hard. It would serve Mummy right if she came upstairs and found Jeremy James all shrivelled up on the carpet.

Jeremy James lay down on the carpet,

tongue hanging out, hand protecting his eyes from the burning sun and the circling vultures. Then with a shudder he gave one last gasp, and lay perfectly still.

But being dead wasn't much fun either, so he rolled over and over until he reached the bed. There were a lot of things under the bed – building blocks, cars, drawings, picture books. Under the bed was the best place for them. Under the bed they didn't cause any trouble at all. It was only when they came out from under the bed that they made a mess. But if they had to come out, then they had to come out, and so out they came.

A liquorice all-sort packet looked interesting, but failed to rattle when shaken. An old toffee stuck to the bottom of a racing car might have been interesting once, but now with its coat of fluff and dust, it was more mucky than sucky. There was simply nothing but rubbish here, and what was the point of bringing rubbish out into the room. He could throw it all away, of course, but if he threw it away he wouldn't have it any more, and there was no point in *not* having things.

What was that glittering in the corner? Probably silver paper. It had better come out as well. Jeremy James snake-wiggled under the bed, reached out, and grasped a shape that was very familiar and very, very pleasing to the fingers. It was a solid square shape, with deep grooves all the way along and all the way across. It was a shape that brought happiness to the heart and water to the mouth. It was a bar-of-chocolate shape.

Jeremy James wiggle-snaked out from under the bed to examine his treasure. Only in one corner had the silver paper been torn, and there the square of chocolate looked a little faded and dusty, but when he carefully peeled the foil away from the neighbouring square. . .well, it looked good enough to eat. And it was. And so was the square next to it. Would they all be as good?

It must have been at Christmas time, when he'd had so many nice things, and this one must have. . .would this square be all right, too?. . .must have slipped down between bed and wall. . .delicious . . .and hidden itself behind all the rubbish . . . amazing how it kept its flavour. . .

'Have you finished, Jeremy James?' came Mummy's voice from downstairs.

'Just a couple of squares to go!' called Jeremy James.

'What's that?' called Mummy.

'Oh!' said Jeremy James. 'Just a couple more things to put away!'

'Right, I'll be up in a minute!'

A minute! Time for action! Jeremy James put the remaining two squares in his mouth and scrunched them while he scooped up a pile of rubbish and dropped it in the box. On top of this pile of rubbish he dropped a second pile, and then a third. Next came the racing car, lorry, gun and book from the bed, more toys from the floor, the bedside table, the chair – everything piled onto the pile above the pile on the pile. With two seconds to go, as Mummy's footsteps creaked on the top stair, Jeremy James lifted up his bedside rug and spread it neatly over the bulging box.

'That's better,' said Mummy. 'Isn't that better, Jeremy James?'

'Yes, Mummy,' said Jeremy James.

'No rubbish, though?'

'No, Mummy.'

'Did you find any lost treasures?'

'Just a what's-a-name,' said Jeremy James.

'There you are,' said Mummy, 'it's worth keeping your room tidy.'

And she was so pleased with Jeremy James that she gave him three squares of chocolate. Unusually for him, Jeremy James had some difficulty forcing them down, and afterwards he needed two glasses of blackcurrant juice, because tidying was such thirsty work.

When Mummy had gone upstairs to vacuum Jeremy James's room, Daddy poked his head out of his study.

'Have you finished?' he asked Jeremy James.

'Yes,' said Jeremy James.

'So have I,' said Daddy. 'Want to look?'

Daddy's study was very tidy indeed. There were no papers or books or letters to be seen anywhere. On the desk was nothing but the typewriter, there was nothing on the floor, nothing on top of the filing cabinet, nothing on the window ledge.

'Pretty good, eh?' said Daddy. 'You want to know how it's done?'

'How?' asked Jeremy James.

Daddy marched to the built-in cupboard at the back of his study.

'Ta ra!' he sang, and flung open the cupboard door. And inside the cupboard was the biggest mess of papers, books and letters you ever saw.

'You see,' he said, 'these are the tricks you learn as you get older, Jeremy James. Out of sight, out of mind. But don't tell your mother.'

'I won't,' said Jeremy James.

8 Freezing

It was going to be a miserable afternoon. Uncle Jack and Aunt Janet had just arrived, with their daughter Melissa. Melissa was the same age as Jeremy James, and she was worse than tummy ache.

'Haven't you grown!' said Aunt Janet to Jeremy James.

'Yes,' said Jeremy James. It was difficult to think of any other answer.

'Oh, look at the twins!' she cried. 'They're *crawling*!'

Christopher and Jennifer were indeed scrabbling round the living-room and giggling, but what was so special about that? If Jeremy James had crawled round giggling, would anyone have shrieked and clapped their hands? They'd probably have told him to stand up before his knees got dirty.

'Wait till you see them stand,' said Mummy.

At that very moment, Christopher seized hold of a chair leg, and slowly hauled himself to his feet, eyes shining with the effort and the triumph.

'Good! Good!' cried Aunt Janet, clapping again.

Jennifer crawled to Christopher, grabbed his leg, and pulled. Plonk. Down came Christopher, and his triumph crumpled into pain and shock. Out came the tears and the wailing cry. Jennifer sat and watched with an expression of amused interest.

'Jennifer, that's naughty!' said Mummy.

Jennifer smiled sweetly.

'Oh, aren't they gorgeous!' said Aunt Janet.

It was going to be a miserable afternoon.

Uncle Jack patted Jeremy James on the head. 'How's my favourite nephew, then?'

'Very well, thank you,' said Jeremy James.

Uncle Jack usually came up with a coin or two at the end of his visits, and so his questions were worth answering.

The pig-tailed Melissa stood clutching her dolly and watching the twins. In fact, everyone was watching the twins. This might be a good chance to escape before

Mummy spoke the dreaded words: 'Jeremy James, why don't you go and play with Melissa?'

Jeremy James crept out of the living-room, into the hall, up the stairs, and into his room. He was just about to close the door when Mummy's voice rang out:

'Jeremy James!'

'Yes, Mummy?'

'Where are you?'

'Here, Mummy!'

'Why don't you come and play with Melissa?'

It was a question which Jeremy James could have answered in some detail, but while he was still looking for the best way to start his list, Mummy spoke again:

'Melissa, dear, would you like to go up and play with Jeremy James?'

'No,' said Melissa.

'Good,' said Jeremy James.

'Up you go, then,' said Mummy.

'Come on, I'll take you,' said Aunt Janet. And up they came – Mummy, Aunt Janet, Melissa and Dolly.

'What a lovely, tidy room!' said Aunt Janet.

Mummy smiled at Jeremy James, and Jeremy James grimaced at Mummy.

'Do you always keep it so tidy?' asked Aunt Janet.

'Only when Mummy makes me,' said Jeremy James.

'Now you'd better play in here till it stops raining,' said Mummy. 'So have a nice game.'

Mummy and Aunt Janet went downstairs again, leaving Jeremy James and Melissa to eye each other like cat and dog.

'What are we going to play?' asked Melissa.

'I don't know,' said Jeremy James. 'What about ludo?'

'I don't like ludo,' said Melissa.

'Do you like racing cars?' asked Jeremy James.

'No,' said Melissa.

'We could play cowboys,' said Jeremy James.

'I don't like cowboys,' said Melissa.

And Melissa didn't like guns or lorries or jungles or drawing or wrestling or spacecraft or anything in this whole wide world except. . .

'I like Freezing.'

'What's Freezing?'

'You hide something, and the other person has to find it, and you tell him if he's freezing, or cold, or warm, or hot.'

'Sounds silly to me.'

'That's the only game I like. If we can't

play Freezing, I won't play anything, and I'll tell Mummy, so there.'

'Oh, all right,' said Jeremy James. 'Who's going to do the hiding?'

'You hide something, and I'll go out of the room till you're ready.'

Melissa and her dolly left the room. She did not close the door behind her, and Jeremy James could see her peeping through the crack between the hinges. He marched to the door and slammed it shut.

'Hope you got your nose caught!' he said. 'Rotten cheat!'

Now, the first thing to choose was the object to hide – something nice and small. Like a sweet wrapper. There was a sweet wrapper under his pillow. Where was the best place to hide it? On top of the wardrobe. She'd *never* think of looking up there.

'Are you ready yet?' asked Melissa from outside.

'No,' said Jeremy James.

He dragged his bedside chair across to the wardrobe, clambered up, put the sweet wrapper in the dust, got down, dragged the chair back to the bed, and sat in it.

'Ready!' he said.

In came Melissa.

'You'll never find it,' said Jeremy James.

'Oh yes I will,' said Melissa, and walked straight to the wardrobe. 'Am I warm?'

'Yes. . .well. . .sort of,' said Jeremy James.

'How warm?' asked Melissa.

'Very warm, I suppose,' said Jeremy James.

'Bring the chair here,' said Melissa.

'What for?' asked Jeremy James.

'Because,' said Melissa, 'I want to see what's on top of the wardrobe.'

'You cheated!' said Jeremy James. 'You were looking!'

'No I wasn't,' said Melissa. 'You closed the door, so how could I look?'

'You made a hole in it!'

'I didn't!'

'You did!'

'I didn't! Shall I tell you how I knew?'

'I don't care,' said Jeremy James. 'Rotten cheat!'

'I heard you moving the chair,' said Melissa.

'It's a silly game anyway,' said Jeremy James. 'I'm not playing silly games.'

'I bet I can hide something where you won't find it,' said Melissa.

'I bet you can't,' said Jeremy James.

'All right,' said Melissa, 'you go out of the room and close the door.'

Jeremy James went out of the room, and closed the door. Then he stood up against the door and put his ear close to it. Not a sound. He bent down to try and see underneath, but the carpet blocked his view. He looked for a hole or a crack, but there were no holes or cracks. All the same, he'd soon find whatever she hid wherever she hid it.

'Ready!' called Melissa.

In marched Jeremy James. Melissa was standing with her dolly beside the wardrobe. Jeremy James headed straight for the wardrobe and Melissa moved out of the way.

'Well?' asked Jeremy James.

'Freezing,' said Melissa.

Jeremy James walked confidently to the other side of the room where he had his box of toys. Melissa returned to the wardrobe.

'Freezing,' she said.

Jeremy James walked a little less confidently to his bed, and Melissa wandered over to the door.

'Freezing,' she said.

'Aha!' said Jeremy James. There was now only one side of the room where he hadn't been. He crossed to the door, and Melissa stepped aside and stood in front of the wardrobe again.

'Freezing,' she said.

'How can it be freezing?' said Jeremy James. 'I've been . . . ah!'

He had not yet tried the middle of the

room, and hanging down from the ceiling
was the lampshade.

'Clever,' said Jeremy James. 'But not
clever enough.'

He stood below the lamp.

'Freezing,' said Melissa.

Jeremy James stood in the middle of the
room and scratched his head. This was not
so easy. If it wasn't on any side or in the
middle, where could it be? Unless . . . could
she have put it outside?

Melissa was still in front of the wardrobe, and beside the wardrobe was the
window. Jeremy James took a cautious
step towards the window, then looked
inquiringly at Melissa.

'A tiny bit warmer,' she said.

He took another step.

'A tiny bit warmerer,' she said.

Jeremy James took two more steps, and
Melissa moved aside.

'Colder,' she said.

Jeremy James frowned. How could it be
colder when he'd actually gone nearer?
Maybe she'd made a mistake. He went all
the way to the window.

'Freezing,' she said.

Jeremy James was fed up. Wherever he
went he was freezing, and even when he
was warmer he was soon colder and it just
didn't make sense.

'Give up?' asked Melissa.

'It's a stupid game,' said Jeremy James. 'I don't care where you've hidden whatever it is.'

'It's one of your little racing cars,' said Melissa.

'Couldn't care less,' said Jeremy James.

'Then I won't tell you where it is,' said Melissa.

'Where is it?' asked Jeremy James.

'It's in Dolly's knickers,' said Melissa, pulling Dolly's skirt up to reveal her triumph.

'That's not fair!' said Jeremy James.

'Yes it is,' said Melissa, 'and I told you you'd never find it.'

'I'm not playing any more stupid games!' said Jeremy James, and pulled his lorry out of the box and sent it hurtling across the room into the wall below the window.

When Mummy came to fetch them for tea, Melissa was quietly combing Dolly's hair, and Jeremy James was quietly drawing a little girl. The little girl in his drawing was flat on her back with a big dagger in her chest.

'What good children,' said Mummy. 'Had a nice game, then?'

'Yes,' said Melissa.

'No,' said Jeremy James.

Uncle Jack, Aunt Janet, Melissa and Dolly finally left, in a flurry of kisses and heart-sinking promises to come again soon. It had indeed been a thoroughly miserable afternoon, but two bright things had come out of it. One was the shiny fifty-pence piece that Uncle Jack slipped into Jeremy James's hand as they said goodbye. Fifty pence was worth being miserable for. And the other consolation was the thought that it might be fun to have a game of Freezing with Timothy from next door. Especially if they each hid a packet of sweets and played finders keepers.

9   The crooked house

Mummy had decided that the whole family should have their photograph taken. Mummy and Daddy themselves had, of course, taken lots of photographs – whole albums of them. Mummy was very good at photographing upwards – her photos were always full of huge expanses of sky, tree-tops, or the roofs of houses, and if they were taken indoors she was good at catching ceilings and the tops of walls. Then occasionally she would also manage to catch somebody's face, usually right down at the bottom of the picture.

Daddy, on the other hand, photographed downwards. He was a specialist in feet, lawns, roads, and carpets. Legs and even bodies could often be seen in his pictures, but faces were a rarity. If he did photo-graph a face, it usually ended at the mouth or nose. You hardly ever saw a pair of eyes in one of Daddy's pictures.

And so Mummy persuaded Daddy to make an appointment with a Mr Pringle, who was a real photographer and could actually get faces into the middle of his pictures. He lived a little way out of town, but the Smyth-Fortescues from next door had been to him, and Mummy reckoned that if he could photograph Timothy, he could photograph anyone.

Mr Pringle had wavy grey hair and a smooth pink face, and he wore a mauve jacket. He didn't say 'photograph' but 'photogwaph', and he walked with a heavy limp, as if one of his legs was twice as heavy as the other. He lived in a tiny cottage, whose doorways were so low that Daddy had to duck his head to get through them. The little rooms were full of pictures and ornaments, and there seemed hardly enough space for anyone to sit down. Not that the family were invited to sit down – they simply passed through, on their way to what looked like a barn in the back garden. The barn was what Mr Pringle called his studio, and it was full of lights, pictures, screens and cameras.

'Have you ever been inside a studio before, Jewemy James?' asked Mr Pringle.

'I don't think so,' said Jeremy James. 'And why do you talk so funny?'

'Well,' said Mr Pringle, 'I can't pwon-

ounce my 'r's. Some childwen can't pwon-
ounce *r* either, but I suppose you can.'

'Yes,' said Jeremy James.

'Lucky you,' said Mr Pringle.

'And why do you walk so funny?' asked
Jeremy James.

'Sh, Jeremy James,' said Mummy, her
face going a little red.

'It's all wight,' said Mr Pringle. 'He's
quite wight to ask. I can't walk pwoperly
because I've lost a leg.'

'Does that mean your leg is dead?' asked
Jeremy James. 'Or did you just drop it
somewhere?'

Jeremy James had once met a lady who
had lost her husband and son, and he'd
spent hours looking for them till he was
told that 'lost' meant 'dead'. Now he wasn't
sure when lost meant dead and when lost
meant lost (as in 'I've lost a piece of chocolate') — but apparently Mr Pringle's leg
was neither dead lost nor lost lost, but had
simply been taken away after an accident.

'Where did they put your leg after they'd
taken it away?' asked Jeremy James.

'To tell you the twuth,' said Mr Pringle,
'I don't know. Maybe they buwied it.'

Jeremy James would have liked to ask
more questions about the lost leg, but Mr
Pringle now busied himself in the studio.
He slid a white screen across the back of

a platform at one end, then he placed two chairs on the platform for Mummy and Daddy to sit on. Mummy was to hold Christopher, Daddy was to hold Jennifer, and Jeremy James was to stand in between. It was all very simple, until Mr Pringle started messing about with the lights. He turned them on, he turned them off, he moved them here, he moved them there, he made them lighter, he made them darker, he put them lower, he put them higher... and all the time he kept saying: 'We must get it wight, mustn't we?'

'Or at least,' said Daddy to Mummy, 'black and wight.'

Jeremy James decided that photography was boring, Jennifer decided it was funny (perhaps because of the silly faces Daddy was pulling), and Christopher decided it was the perfect moment to do his Number Two. There was a sudden loud and rather rude noise, he wriggled back stiffly in Mummy's arms, and the studio was soon filled with a smell that had nothing to do with photography.

'Oh dear,' said Mummy, 'I think I'd better change him, or we'll never be able to smile.'

Mr Pringle caught a whiff and swiftly opened the door for Mummy.

Jeremy James followed Mummy and

Christopher out of the studio, but while they went on through the house, he decided to do a bit of exploring. He wandered round the side of the studio, and found himself in a strange little garden full of flowers and gnomes and toy animals. At the very top of this garden, up a crazy paving path, stood a tiny crooked house which looked as if it had come straight out of a book of fairy-tales. It was painted in bright colours, and its roof, chimney, windows and door were all set at different angles. It was the kind of house you simply had to go and have a look at.

Jeremy James tried to peep through its windows, but they were covered on the inside with black blinds, so he couldn't see anything. Next he tried the door, and to his delight it opened. He looked inside, but it was still too dark for him to see anything.

'Is anybody there?' he asked.

Nobody said anything.

'Anybody at home?' asked Jeremy James.

Complete silence.

Witches lived in houses like these, so you had to be careful. It could be the house of the witch that took Mr Pringle's leg away after his accident. Mr Pringle might even have come here looking for his leg

and not found it because it was too dark for him to find anything. Or because he was too frightened even to look. After all, not everyone is brave enough actually to go *inside* a witch's house. Jeremy James wasn't even certain that *he* was brave enough.

'Are you sure you're not at home?' asked Jeremy James.

No reply.

If a witch was at home, she'd probably say she was at home. And if she was asleep, she would be snoring. Jeremy James stood still and quiet. Not a sound. He pushed the door open as wide as it could go. Still not a sound.

'I can see you,' he said. 'You're hiding behind the door!'

Not a murmur, not a movement.

Jeremy James took a deep breath, and stepped inside the crooked house. He stood there for a moment, waiting to be bonked on the head, but nothing happened. In the light from the doorway he could now see some tables and stands with things hanging on them. No sign of a leg, but that could be hidden in the shadows. He needed more light. Jeremy James boldly marched to one of the blinds. It was attached by a simple loop on a hook, and in no time at all, Jeremy James had raised both blinds and the sunlight was streaming all over the crooked house. It revealed nothing but long strips of shiny film hanging on the stands, photographs on the walls, basins of water with papers in them. . . no witches, no gingerbread men, no toys, no magic potions, and no lost legs. It was all a big disappointment.

'Jeremy James!' That was Daddy's voice, calling from the garden. Jeremy James walked out of the crooked house.

'Ah, there you are!' said Daddy. 'I thought you'd gone with Mummy. Nice little house that, isn't it?'

'No,' said Jeremy James. 'It's boring.'

'Anyway, come on,' said Daddy, 'Mr Pringle's waiting for us.'

And the 'photogwaphing' proved to be as boring as the rest of the afternoon.

A week later, Mr Pringle brought the photographs round to Mummy and Daddy. Even Jeremy James had to agree that they were beautiful pictures. Somehow everyone had managed to look happy, handsome and smart, and seeing those handsome happy faces, you would never have thought of moving lights, pooey nappies and yawning boredom.

'I'm glad you like them,' said Mr Pringle. 'You know, a tewwible thing happened that day you came.'

'What was that?' asked Daddy.

'Somebody bwoke into my dark woom. They let all the blinds up, and all my photogwaphs were wuined – absolutely wuined. A whole week's work destwoyed.'

'Oh dear,' said Mummy. 'Who would do an awful thing like that?'

'I expect it was childwen,' said Mr Pringle. 'They didn't take anything. Just wuined the photogwaphs.'

A thought struck Jeremy James. At the same time, the same thought struck Daddy.

'Mr Pringle,' said Daddy. 'Your dark room – it isn't that little crooked house in the garden, is it?'

'That's wight,' said Mr Pringle.

'Oh!' said Daddy.

And 'Oh!' thought Jeremy James.

'In that case, Mr Pringle,' said Daddy, 'perhaps you and I could have a little chat.'

Daddy and Mr Pringle went out, with Daddy looking worried and Mr Pringle looking puzzled, and they left Jeremy James looking uncomfortable, and Mummy looking at the photographs.

'Mummy,' said Jeremy James. 'What's a dark woom?'

'A dark *room*,' said Mummy. 'It's a place where photographers develop their photographs. They make the film into photos.'

'Why is it dark?' asked Jeremy James.

'Because light ruins the film,' said Mummy.

'Oh!' said Jeremy James.

'Do you know something about Mr Pringle's dark room?' asked Mummy.

'Well,' said Jeremy James, 'I think I may have been there.'

Before Mummy could ask any more questions, Daddy came back with Mr Pringle, and Daddy was looking embarrassed, and Mr Pringle was looking pleased.

'Is everything all right?' asked Mummy.

'You might say,' said Daddy, 'that the answer is in the negative.'

When Mr Pringle had gone, Daddy explained to Mummy that Jeremy James had unfortunately been exploring in Mr Pringle's garden, and he then explained to Jeremy James that other people's closed doors were best left closed.

'I was only looking for Mr Pringle's leg,' said Jeremy James.

Mummy and Daddy both agreed that Jeremy James couldn't have known what was behind the door, and maybe Mr Pringle should have kept it locked, knowing there were children about.

'Anyway,' said Daddy, 'let's have a good

look at these photographs. Because believe me, they're worth their weight in gold.'

'How much did you give him?' asked Mummy.

Jeremy James gasped when he heard the sum.

'You could buy a million ice creams with that!' he cried.

'That,' said Daddy, 'is the price of development. His, and yours.'

10   Birthday twins

Tomorrow would be the twins' first birthday.

'I wish,' said Jeremy James at the breakfast table, 'that I could have a gerbil for their birthday.'

'Why,' asked Daddy from behind the newspaper, 'should *you* have a gerbil for *their* birthday?'

'Well Richard's got a gerbil,' said Jeremy James. 'And it runs round a wheel and it eats paper and it's clever and nice and I wish I could have a gerbil.'

'Yes, I understand that,' said Daddy. 'What I don't understand is why *you* should have a gerbil for the *twins*' birthday.'

'Because,' said Jeremy James, 'people give people presents on people's birthdays.'

Mummy explained to Jeremy James that it was only the people that had birthdays who were given presents. Jeremy James explained to Mummy that at the birthday parties he'd been to, *everybody* was given a present, and the present he would like to be given was a gerbil.

'And what present are you going to give the twins?' asked Mummy.

This was a problem that Jeremy James had been trying hard not to think about. The trouble was, his pocket money had all gone to the sweetshop, and Uncle Jack's fifty pence had gone the same way, and how do you get people presents if you haven't got any money?

Jeremy James put this question to Mummy and Daddy.

'It's a good question,' said Daddy.

Jeremy James was pleased that Daddy liked his question, and he waited for the answer. But the answer didn't come. Daddy simply put his eyes back on his newspaper and his lips back on his cup of tea. Daddy wasn't very good at solving problems anyway.

'Mummy,' said Jeremy James, 'if you hadn't got any money, how would you buy presents?'

'If I knew that I had to buy presents,' said Mummy, 'I'd make sure I saved some money for them. Instead of spending it all at the sweetshop.'

Mummy was good at solving problems. Only her solutions didn't always help Jeremy James.

Jeremy James decided to ask the twins for a solution, and the solution he had in mind seemed a rather clever one.

'You don't really want a birthday present, do you?' he said to Christopher, while Mummy was bathing Jennifer.

'Hihihi!' gurgled Christopher, standing up in his cot and shaking the sides.

'Say no,' said Jeremy James.

'Hihihi!' said Christopher.

'Not hihihi,' said Jeremy James. 'No. Say NO. NO-O-O.'

'Hihihi,' said Christopher.

Christopher was just like Daddy when it came to solving problems.

Ten minutes later, when Mummy was bathing Christopher, Jeremy James put his suggestion to Jennifer.

'You don't want a birthday present, do you?' he said. 'Just say no.'

'Ball,' said Jennifer.

'What?' said Jeremy James.

'Ball,' said Jennifer. 'Boo. . .Jem Jem. . .Wiffer. . .'

'No,' said Jeremy James. 'Say no.'

Jennifer laughed. 'Jem Jem!' she said. 'Wiffer. . .ball. . .Jeffer. . .boo.'

Jennifer was just like Mummy when it came to solving problems.

In the course of the morning, Jeremy James had two more ideas about how to escape from present-buying. The first was to fall ill. Nobody can buy presents when they're ill. But the only time he'd been ill, it had been through eating too many liquorice all-sorts, and to eat too many liquorice all-sorts he would first of all need to *have* too many liquorice all-sorts, and in his present state of coinlessness he could not even afford one liquorice all-sort let alone too many.

The second idea seemed more possible. He explained it to Mummy and Daddy at lunch.

'If you gave me the gerbil as my present *before* the twins' birthday,' he said, '*I* could give it to *them* as *their* present, couldn't I?'

'What gerbil?' asked Daddy.

The idea began to seem less possible.

'What would Christopher and Jennifer do with a gerbil?' asked Mummy.

The idea didn't seem possible at all.

In the course of the afternoon, Jeremy James had no further ideas except the idea that other people's birthdays were a bad idea.

At tea Mummy saw the worried expression on Jeremy James's face and she told him that he didn't really have to buy the twins a present at all. She said they were too young to understand about birthdays anyway. But Mummy was always saying Jeremy James was too young to understand things, and he knew that he wasn't. He understood everything, except why grown-ups thought children were too young to understand things they did understand or would understand if they were properly explained. The twins certainly understood about birthdays, and if they wanted a present and he didn't buy them a present, they certainly wouldn't buy *him* a present when it was *his* birthday.

No ideas came into Jeremy James's head that evening (perhaps because he was busy watching a film). And no ideas came into his head that night (perhaps because he was busy sleeping). But the following morning, when he woke up, there in his brain lay the answer, and it was so simple that he wondered why he hadn't thought of it before. Mummy had been completely wrong. Not only did the twins understand about birthdays, but they'd even solved Jeremy James's problem for him.

With a little giggle of excitement, Jeremy James leapt out of bed, and a moment later there was a sound rather like a building falling down. This was followed by a good deal of banging and scraping, and when Mummy poked her nose through the door to see what was going on, she saw Jeremy James sitting beside his upside-down toy box, surrounded by toys.

'What on earth are you doing?' she asked.

Jeremy James thought for a moment.

'Tidying,' he said.

'Ah,' said Mummy. 'Good.' And off she went to prepare breakfast.

By the time breakfast was ready, Jeremy James had finished banging and scraping, and he had also finished a long session of rustling. His smile had spread all over his face much as his toys had spread all over the floor, because he had found what he had been looking for. When he went downstairs, he felt light enough to fly. It was almost worth having problems just for the pleasure of finding the solutions.

When Mummy and Daddy had dressed Christopher and Jennifer in their new birthday clothes and had placed their new giant teddy bears in their arms, Jeremy James raced to his room and returned with two parcels. One of them was small and

round and wrapped in an old paper bag. The other was large and square and wrapped in two old paper bags.

'Boo!' said Jennifer, as she took the bags off her present. 'Jeffer. . .boo!' And a 'boo' it was. One of Jeremy James's old picture books which had been buried at the bottom of his toy box.

'Hihihi!' said Christopher, as he took the paper bag off his present.

'Wiffer. . .ball!' cried Jennifer, glancing across at her brother. And a ball it was. A bouncy rubber ball which Jeremy James sometimes played with in the garden. It was a ball he would rather like to play with again, so perhaps he might borrow it from Christopher later on.

'Very nice presents,' said Mummy.

'Well done, Jeremy James,' said Daddy.

'It's just what they wanted,' said Jeremy James. 'They told me when I asked them.'

'Talking of what people want,' said Daddy, 'there's something up in our bedroom that might interest you, Jeremy James.'

Jeremy James broke the world record for up-the-stairs-and-into-the-bedroom. On the dressing-table was a large cage of glass and metal, and inside it was a wheel. Near the wheel was a ladder, and near the ladder was a swing. And near the swing was a bowl of water, and near the bowl of water was a pile of sawdust. And in the sawdust, huddled together and fast asleep, were the tiny furry bodies of. . .TWO GERBILS!

Jeremy James let out a whoop that would have turned an oak tree into sawdust. TWO GERBILS!

'We thought one would be lonely on its own,' said Daddy from the bedroom doorway. 'Happy Unbirthday, Jeremy James.'

'TWO GERBILS!' cried Jeremy James for the third time.

'What are you going to call them, then?' asked Mummy from behind Daddy.

Jeremy James knew straight away what the gerbils were going to be called.

'Wiffer and Jeffer,' he said.

Mummy and Daddy laughed.

'Why Wiffer and Jeffer?' asked Daddy.

'Because,' said Jeremy James, 'they're twins and they're clever and nice and thank you and Richard's only got one gerbil and Wiffer and Jeffer are the best present in the whole world. . .'

There was no doubt that birthdays were a good idea after all. And so were twins.